Welcome to the world of
MASK
MOBILE ARMOURED STRIKE KOMMAND

Imagine a world where there is more to
reality than meets the eye. Where illusion
and deception team up with
man and machine to create a world of
sophisticated vehicles and weaponry,
manned by agents and counter-agents.

Venice Menace

The MASK mission: to thwart VENOM's evil
plans in one of the world's most beautiful
cities – with the assistance of Scott Trakker and
his courageous robot companion T-Bob.

The third sensational **MASK** adventure.

MATT TRAKKER – SPECTRUM

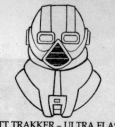

MATT TRAKKER – ULTRA FLASH

BRAD TURNER – HOCUS POCUS

HONDO MACLEAN – BLASTER

BUDDIE HAWKES – PENETRATOR

BRUCE SATO – LIFTER

DUSTY HAYES – BACKLASH

ALEX SECTOR – JACKRABBIT

CLIFF DAGGER – THE TORCH

MILES MAYHEM – VIPER

SLY RAX – STILETTO

MASK

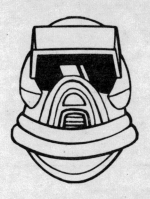

VENICE MENACE

novelisation by
Kenneth Harper

Illustrated by Bruce Hogarth

KNIGHT BOOKS
Hodder and Stoughton

With special thanks to Bruce Hogarth and David Lewis
Management for their great help and hard work.

Mask TM and the associated trade marks are the property of
Kenner Parker Toys Inc. (KPT) 1986
Text copyright © Kenneth Harper 1986
Illustrations copyright © Bruce Hogarth 1986

First published by Knight Books 1986

British Library C.I.P.

Harper, Kenneth
    Venice Menace.—(Mask; 3)
    I. Title   II. Hogarth, Bruce   III. Series
    823'.914[J] PZ7

    ISBN 0-340-39892-2

Printed and bound in Great Britain for
Hodder and Stoughton Paperbacks, a
division of Hodder and Stoughton Ltd.,
Mill Road, Dunton Green, Sevenoaks,
Kent (Editorial Office: 47 Bedford Square,
London WC1B 3DP) by
Cox and Wyman Ltd., Reading
Photoset by Rowland Phototypesetting Ltd
Bury St Edmunds, Suffolk

ONE

Venice basked lazily in the afternoon sunshine. The five-domed cathedral of St Mark looked truly magnificent, the Palace of the Doge was as stately as ever and the famous Bridge of Sighs was at its best in the bright light. Tourists flocked to the huge St. Mark's Square or explored the art galleries and the shops.

But the main attraction was the water.

The city was built on numerous small islands divided into two groups by the Grand Canal which is also the main thoroughfare. Three great bridges crossed it – Scalzi, Rialto and Accademia – and about a hundred and fifty smaller canals branched off it.

Venice was truly water-borne.

Since the easiest way to see the city was by canal,

Matt Trakker cruised along in a sleek power boat that left a curling wake behind it. Matt was at the helm. One of his MASK colleagues, Jacques Lafleur, was with him in the craft.

Jacques was a tall, handsome, smiling French-Canadian. Like Matt, he was wearing civilian dress and seemed to be just another tourist. He was very impressed with the beautiful architecture all around him.

When he spoke, his voice had a distinctive French accent.

'Venice is very different from anything I ever saw in Canada, *mon ami*,' he observed.

Matt nodded. 'The city of canals is different from any other place in the world. I love it here.'

'Me too.'

'It's so quiet and peaceful.'

A great swishing noise contradicted him.

'What's that?' he asked.

He got his answer immediately. It was T-Bob.

The short, round, comical-looking robot had converted to ski-bob mode to take to the water. Feet apart and floating on the surface, he was powered along by his wheel. Sitting astride him and enjoying every moment of the ride was Scott Trakker, an alert, mischievous boy with a tremendous sense of fun. As they hared along, they sent up a bank of foam across the canal.

Scott waved cheerily to Matt and Jacques.

'Come on! You guys are too slow.'

7

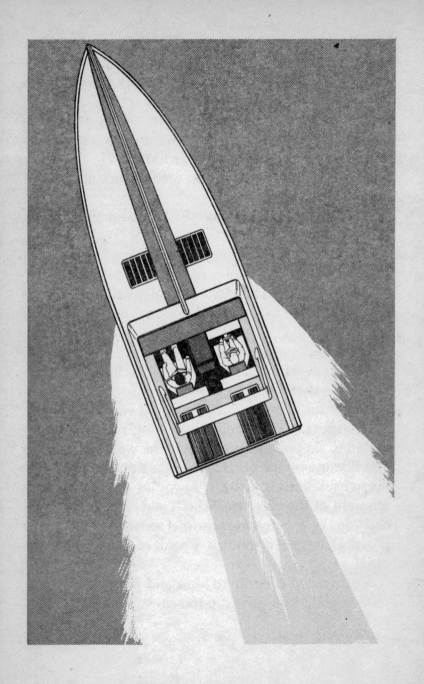

'Take it easy, son,' advised Matt. 'It's not a race.'

'I want some action, Dad.'

'Full speed ahead!' shouted T-Bob.

'Just look at him go!' said Jacques with a grin.

The robot accelerated and went on past the power boat. He was about to streak right away, when he seemed to hit something just below the water line. T-Bob came to a dramatic halt and vibrated like a knife stuck in wood.

Scott was taken completely by surprise.

'Wow!!!!'

He was hurled through the air at speed.

SPLASH!!!!

He hit the water with a resounding smack.

'Can he swim?' asked Jacques in alarm, reaching for a lifebelt.

'Yes,' reassured Matt. 'I taught him years ago.'

Scott came up for air and spat out some water.

'Hey, T-Bob!' he complained. 'What's the matter with you?'

'Nothing,' said the robot.

'Then why'd you stop?'

'I *didn't* stop.'

'Well, it sure *felt* like it,' argued the boy.

T-Bob was sitting in the water, glancing around in a state of confusion. He strained hard to move forward but could not budge. The water around him looked the same as that in any other stretch of the canal. Yet he was immobilised as if held in some thick glue.

'I'm . . . I'm stuck!' he piped.

Matt Trakker piloted the boat up alongside Scott, and Jacques leaned over to grasp the boy under the arms. In one fluent move, the French-Canadian lifted the dripping figure out of the water and put him down safely in the stern.

'Thanks, Jacques,' said Scott.

'My pleasure,' returned the other.

'What happened to T-Bob?'

'He must have hit a sand-bar.'

Matt eased the boat across to the robot. T-Bob was still struggling to get free but something just below the surface seemed to be holding him securely.

Matt scratched his head in bewilderment.

'I don't get it,' he said.

'Neither do I!' wailed T-Bob.

'There's no sand-bar around here. The water's too deep.'

'Aw,' decided Scott. 'He's just playing one of his jokes. Come on, T-Bob.'

'I wish I could,' moaned the robot.

Jacques leaned over to take a firm grip on T-Bob.

'Wow! He's heavy!'

Powerful and determined, Jacques tightened his grip and hauled the robot up by the arms which telescoped out to maximum length before he finally rose out of the water. He did not come alone.

They were all astonished at what they saw.

'Jeepers!' exclaimed Scott.

'What *is* it?' wondered Jacques.

'That's the last thing I expected,' confessed Matt.

'Help!' shrieked T-Bob.

The robot was stuck up to his waist in a big, clear, jelly-like mass. It was irregular, about one metre in diameter, and it looked like a chunk of ice except that it had the rubbery quality of stiff gelatine.

T-Bob instantly flew into a panic.

'It's a jellyfish!' he cried. 'I'm being eaten alive by a giant jellyfish!'

Jacques set him and the blob down in the boat. Matt examined the substance, poking at it with a pocket knife. He tried to soothe the robot with his findings.

'It's not a jellyfish, T-Bob. And it's not alive.'

'Thank goodness for that!'

'But it *is* very interesting.'

'It'd be more interesting if only it'd let me go!'

Matt used his knife to cut around T-Bob so that he was freed. The robot scrambled away from the blob and stared at it in terror. Matt sliced off a small piece and studied it in the palm of his hand. He squeezed it and tried to tear it into smaller chunks. It resisted.

'It's like gelatine,' he said, 'but it's extremely dense and strong. It just won't tear.'

'What was it doing in the canal?' asked Jacques.

'Waiting to make a meal of *me*!' groaned T-Bob.

'Let's take it back and analyse it,' suggested Matt.

'Could we just throw it overboard and forget about it?' said the robot. 'Just this once?'

'No,' replied Matt. 'We have to investigate.'

12

'It could be important,' added Jacques.

'That's why I want you to sling it back,' quavered T-Bob. 'It's important to me that that thing doesn't jump over here and start to gobble me up again.'

He started to shiver and the others laughed good-humouredly.

The power boat headed back along the canal.

Five minutes later, the boat had been lifted out on to a ramp and the four of them were on the landing stage. Parked nearby was the Volcano Van, a large, steel vehicle with all kinds of hidden gadgets. Matt and Jacques lifted the blob out of the boat and carried it over to the van. When they had put it in the back, they locked the double doors behind it. It was now safe and sound.

Scott tried to make T-Bob understand.

'We have to check out anything suspicious, T-Bob.'

'Why?'

'Dad's sources say that VENOM might be operating here.'

'In Venice!'

'Afraid so!'

'That's all I need,' protested the robot. 'First, that jellyfish tried to swallow me. Now, you say that VENOM are here to plot their dark deeds. Why did we *come* to Venice?'

'To have fun, of course.'

'It's no fun being attacked.'

'And it's no fun being thrown into the water,'

14

argued the boy. 'But I'm not upset by it, am I?'

'You didn't get attacked by that rubber iceberg, though!'

'It's probably quite harmless, T-Bob.'

'Harmless! You try having it around *your* legs!'

Matt called them over and they got into Volcano van.

Jacques drove them back towards the hotel. Scott had been able to dry himself with a towel in the boat so he had got over the shock of being pitched into the water. But T-Bob kept nattering on about his terrible experience with the blob.

'It's like Jaws!' he said. 'Without any teeth.'

'We'll soon have it analysed,' promised Matt.

'Wonder what it could possibly be?' said Jacques.

The two men knew it was their duty to check it out. As members of the MASK team, they were dedicated professionals involved in a non-stop fight against crime and evil. There was something very odd about the substance and it might just have a connection with their arch-enemy–

Vicious Evil Network of Mayhem.

VENOM!

The van pulled up outside the hotel and they all got out. Thunder Hawk, Matt's own special vehicle, was parked nearby. He and Jacques went around to the back of the van to unload the blob. When they unlocked the double doors, however, they got a shock.

The big chunk of gelatine had vanished.

All that was left was a tiny pool of water.
T-Bob was the first to speak.
'It's gone!'

TWO

The four of them were totally baffled and stood there with mouths wide open. When the blob went into the rear of the van, it had been so big, solid and permanent. It seemed impossible that it had melted down to such a little puddle.

Where had it gone?

Before they could even begin to answer the question, they were distracted by a loud commotion. Boat horns sounded, klaxons went off, machinery whirled and many voices were raised. The noise was coming from another stretch of the canal.

'What's going on?' asked Jacques with interest.

'I aim to find out,' said Matt. 'Come on.'

'I don't want to go back to the canal again,' protested T-Bob.

'Why not?' challenged Scott.

'Because there might be another jellyfish there.'

'Don't be silly, T-Bob,' said the boy.

'You're safe with us,' promised Matt.

'Yes,' teased Jacques. 'We'll make sure that you're not tossed back into the canal as bait for another rubber-toothed monster!'

They went off laughing down the street.

Reluctantly, T-Bob followed behind them.

When they reached the canal, they found an excited crowd gathered there. Men, women and children lined the bank and peered into the water. Whatever was in there was causing immense curiosity.

Matt and Jacques were tall enough to look over the heads of the others but Scott could see nothing. With a single lift, he was hoisted up on to Matt's shoulders so that he had a grandstand view of the proceedings. He whistled appreciatively.

'Whew! This is just great!'

'What's going on?' called T-Bob from ground level.

'Come on up and take a look.'

'Okay.'

The robot extended his telescopic legs and rose above the heads of the crowd. Like Scott, he could now see what was happening.

There was a bridge across the canal. Parked in the middle of it was a large, mobile crane, mounted on a truck. It was being operated by the driver, a burly Italian in trousers and a sleeveless vest.

The crane had a huge claw for lifting things and it

was being used to pull a gondola out of the canal. Other gondolas floated nearby and the boatmen watched with fascination.

When the empty gondola came clear of the water, a vast glob of gelatinous substance could be seen clinging to it. T-Bob quailed when he recognised the stuff. It was the same jelly-like thing which had stuck to him. This time, however, it was so big that it blocked the whole width of the canal. A long traffic jam had built up and impatient boatmen were using their horns.

The crane's motor groaned as it strained under the weight of its load and the driver had to use full power. Very slowly, the gondola and its attached blob were winched right up.

'That's the same goo *we* found,' noted Scott.

'It's the biggest jellyfish in the world,' said T-Bob.

'We need a sample, Matt,' suggested Jacques.

'Yes,' agreed the other. 'Quick, T-Bob. I need a jar or something to keep it in. See what you can do.'

'Coming up!'

The robot opened his compartment and took out a jar with a screw lid. He handed it to Matt with a weak joke:

'I can hardly contain my excitement.'

'Thanks,' said Matt.

He moved on to the bridge and hung over it so that he could cut a small slice of the blob off. When the gelatine was in his jar, he screwed the lid shut. He showed it to Jacques and held it up to the light. They could see right through the substance.

'We'll make sure *this* fish doesn't get away, Jacques.'

'Yes, Matt.'

'I can't wait to get it analysed.'

Jacques noticed something and yelled a warning.

'Look out! It's coming loose!'

The crane was still holding the gondola aloft but the gelatine was coming unstuck from the boat. It made a loud sucking noise as it parted from the gondola then it dropped back into the canal with an enormous splash.

Everyone was thoroughly soaked.

'Not again!' complained Scott.

'Yow!' added T-Bob. 'That was more than a drop in the bucket!'

The crane operator was getting plenty of advice.

'Lift it out again,' yelled someone.

'Don't leave it in the canal!' shouted another.

'It'll only cause more trouble,' urged a third.

Setting the gondola down on the bank, the driver made the crane swing out over the water again. The great claw descended down into the water and its steel teeth closed with a clang. When the claw resurfaced, however, it was empty.

The cupboard was bare!

'Where did it go?' demanded the crane operator.

'It must be down there somewhere,' argued Matt.

'I'll take a look,' volunteered one of the gondoliers.

He was a short, dark man in a striped vest, light trousers and a straw boater. He guided his gondola out to the spot where the blob had disappeared and he

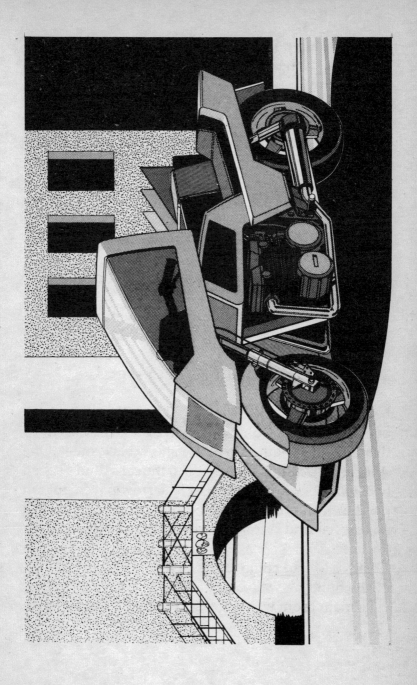

used his long pole to prod the water all around him. He shook his head firmly.

'It's gone.'

'Are you sure?' asked the crane operator.

'There's nothing here.'

The news set the crowd off into a buzz of speculation and they all gazed down at the canal. Everyone was mystified.

Matt Trakker held up his jar.

'Well, at least we saved our sample.'

'*Did* we, Dad?' gulped Scott.

'Where is it?' asked Jacques.

The jar was empty but for a small amount of water.

'It's vanished again!' said Matt.

T-Bob could not resist another weak pun.

'It couldn't have gotten out,' he chirped. 'The lid wasn't even *ajar*!'

They all groaned and rolled their eyes.

Not every part of Venice was filled with architectural beauty. In a dark, dingy, neglected area of the city, a dilapidated building stood in a shady back street. One side of the building fronted on to the canal and a speed boat was docked alongside it. A narrow pavement ran parallel to the canal. Parked on it was a distinctive motorcycle and sidecar. It was Piranha. Owned by Sly Rax.

VENOM had come to the city.

The building was their hideout.

Its main room was large, bare and virtually derelict.

In the corner was a big metal drum that was used for holding chemical liquids. It had special markings and seals all over it as well as a valve. But it also had a small crack in it and a tiny amount of thick, purple fluid oozed out. The fluid glowed with an unearthly light.

Suddenly, a bunched fist slammed down on the drum.

BANG!!!!

Miles Mayhem was not amused.

'Idiots!' he roared. 'The drum is leaking! You could have left a trail leading right to us!'

His anger was directed at two of his henchmen.

Sly Rax was a dark, stocky, cunning man with a moustache and a small tufted beard. He wore narrow goggles across his eyes. Beside him was Bruno Shepard, a giant of a man whose bare arms were covered in rippling muscles. Bald except for a shock of hair in the middle of his head, Bruno had a tough, weathered face and a brutal stare.

'You're fools!' bellowed Mayhem.

'We didn't notice,' said Bruno, sullenly.

Vanessa Warfield strode across to him. She was a tall, shapely young woman with sharp features and a black streak in her hair. Her tone was very sarcastic.

'These boys wouldn't notice if their heads were leaking.'

Rax and Bruno shot her an angry look.

'How were we supposed to notice?' rejoined Rax. 'We had the drum covered in a tarpaulin so that nobody would see it in our boat.'

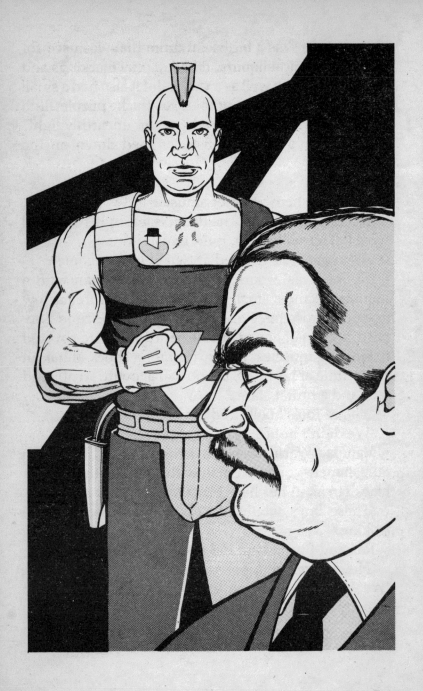

Vanessa went over to the drum and playfully dipped her finger into the purple fluid. It glowed brilliantly when she held it up.

'You didn't notice *this* stuff leaking?' she sneered.

'No,' they admitted in unison.

'Did you suddenly go Venetian blind?' she said.

'Well, it didn't leak much,' Rax pointed out. 'Just a drop here and there.'

'A drop of it is enough,' she warned.

Mayhem was pacing up and down in his irritation.

'You knew this was a super-concentrated formula!'

'Yeah,' conceded Bruno.

'Show them, Vanessa,' ordered Mayhem.

There was a jug of water on the table. Vanessa dipped in the finger that still had the tiny amount of fluid on it. She jiggled it around in the water.

'One drop can effect three cubic metres,' she explained.

She proved her point at once.

The water stiffened into a gel. When she turned the jug over, the blob dropped out on to the table like a solid jelly. She stared down at it with satisfaction as it quivered gently.

Mayhem confronted his men. As leader of VENOM, it was his job to ensure that there were no mistakes made by his agents. He was quite ruthless with anyone who let him down.

'This is one of my finest plans!' he told them. 'If you two cretins foul up on me, I'll throw *you* in the canal.'

25

Rax and Bruno exchanged a surly glance.

'VENOM must succeed this time!' he insisted. 'Understood?'

'Yes, Mayhem,' grunted Rax.

'Yeah,' agreed Bruno.

'Then let's have no more bungling!'

'Or we *all* end up in the drink!' cautioned Vanessa.

Mayhem pushed past the two men and peered furtively through the cracked window. The canal outside was completely deserted. He scratched at his moustache and swung round to face them again.

'You're lucky the gelling effect is only temporary.' He jerked a thumb towards the window. 'Apparently, no one followed your trail.'

'We told you that,' muttered Bruno.

'What do we do now, Mayhem?' said Rax.

'We proceed as planned!'

Mayhem went back to the drum and patted it gently.

He permitted himself an evil chuckle.

'If only MASK knew what we had in here!'

While the VENOM leader was in his hideout, the head of MASK was sitting in Thunder Hawk with Jacques, Scott and T-Bob. Matt Trakker was using the on-board computer to analyse the water in the sample jar. The jar was sitting on the dashboard and numbers were reading out rapidly on the vehicle's monitors.

The computer's female voice was flat and impersonal.

'Analysis of sample: ordinary H_2O with some pollutants.'

'Huh?' gulped T-Bob. 'You mean, that water in the jar is just . . . water in a jar?'

The computer answered his inquiry calmly.

'Chemical pollutants are common in Venice canals. Impossible to isolate cause of gelling effect.'

Matt Trakker switched off the computer and pondered.

'What's the next step?' asked Jacques.

'You and I will scan the computer library to see if this stuff has ever been found before, Jacques.'

'Good idea,' agreed the MASK agent.

'Will you be needing us, Dad?' wondered Scott.

'No. You can do some sightseeing, if you like.'

'Terrific! Thanks, Dad.'

'How will we get around?' said T-Bob. 'I'm not going in the water again if there's any more jellyfish about.'

'We'll hire a boat,' decided the boy.

'That puts the wind in my sails!' piped the robot.

They went off in search of a craft.

If Scott had known what was about to happen, he would never have left the safety of Thunder Hawk. Hiring a boat turned out to be a minor disaster.

But it seemed like a good idea at the time.

THREE

Scott and T-Bob went back to the canal, paid for a boat then stepped into a classic Venetian gondola whose high prow and stern had been painted in bright colours. The flat-bottomed craft looked magnificent and it was the perfect means of seeing Venice at a leisurely pace.

Unfortunately, T-Bob seemed to be in a hurry.

'Okay, I'll drive,' he announced. 'How do you start the motor?'

Scott was in the rear of the boat with a long pole.

'There's no motor,' he explained. 'This is a gondola. A real gondolier pushes it with this long stick.'

The robot jumped towards him and grabbed the pole.

'Leave it to me,' he boasted.

'Are you sure you know what you're doing, T-Bob?'

'Yes. I know all *aboat* this stuff!'

Scott groaned at this latest awful pun.

'Here we go!' shouted the robot. 'Bon voyage!'

He jammed the pole into the water and pushed hard against the canal bottom. The pole lodged itself in thick mud and he was unable to pull it out. As the gondola glided on down the canal, T-Bob was left clinging to the pole. He was only just above the water.

'Eeeek!'

'What's up?' called Scott.

'My stick's stuck! Come back!'

'I can't. You're driving.'

'Do I *look* as if I'm driving?'

The boy heaved a sigh. 'I knew it! Trust you to get it wrong.'

'Come on!' shouted T-Bob. 'Don't be a stick in the mud!'

He began to shake the pole violently to try to work it loose.

'Be careful!' warned Scott.

'I'm pulling it free.'

'But you'll end up in the water.'

'I never thought of that!'

T-Bob stopped moving the pole but it was too late. He had already dislodged it from the mud and it was keeling slowly over. The robot gradually disappeared beneath the dark water.

'I'm going down with my stick!'

His voice became a gurgle as he vanished from sight.

'He's left me up the creek without a paddle,' complained Scott.

The boy lay in the gondola so that he could put both arms over the side of it. He used his hands to paddle the boat laboriously forward. It was hard work and he was soon panting for breath.

T-Bob, meanwhile, had telescoped his legs to full height and walked across the canal bottom. He reached the steps that led to the bank and climbed out. One good shake disposed of most of the water that clung to him and the sun soon dried off the rest. He looked to see where Scott was, then started running.

The boy was approaching a bridge that went over the canal in a graceful arch. It was an ornate structure with wrought-iron handrails on either side. Scott glanced up at it as he was about to pass beneath it. He gulped when he saw T-Bob standing on the bridge with another pole in his hand.

'Oh no!'

'Don't worry, Scott!' yelled the robot. 'I got a new stick. Mind if I drop in?'

'Stay there!' howled the boy.

'Here I come!'

'T-Bob! Don't jump!'

But his friend was already sailing through the air.

'Wheeee!' shouted T-Bob. 'Happy landing!'

He came down hard in the stern of the gondola. Scott was near the prow and he was catapulted upwards as the other end of the boat sank right down. He flew through the air with his eyes shut tight, not daring to look. Suddenly, he stopped. He could not understand why. When he opened his eyes, he saw that he was caught up in a clothes line that was stretched across the canal.

'Where are you?' called T-Bob.

'Up here!'

'Hanging out to dry, are you?'

'Thanks to you!'

The line snapped and it was Scott's turn to fall.

'Ahhhhh!'

As he landed heavily in one end of the gondola, it see-sawed up again at the other end and sent T-Bob shooting off. Holding the pole out in front of him in a horizontal line, he found his progress checked by two of the railings on the bridge. His pole locked into them to form a horizontal bar and he spun around it like a champion gymnast.

On an upswing, he lost his grip and flew through the air once more. Scott braced himself and grabbed hold of the sides of the gondola but T-Bob did not land in the boat this time. With a loud splash, he went into the water, descended all the way to the bottom, then came up again an older and wiser robot.

'This gondola stuff is a little trickier than I thought,' he admitted. 'I haven't quite mastered it yet!'

Two menacing figures emerged from the VENOM hideout and crossed over to the motorcycle and side-

car. Miles Mayhem was wearing his usual smart military uniform. Sly Rax had dark, nondescript clothes on. They stood beside Piranha. Mayhem glanced all around before putting his hand into his pocket to pull out an ancient, tattered piece of parchment.

He gave it to Rax and spoke in a hoarse whisper.

'Here's the map!'

'Right.'

'Now, remember. Venice itself did not exist when that map was drawn up. It's very, very old.'

'I know, I know,' said Rax, impatiently.

'Take good care of it.'

'I will. Stop worrying.'

'No more mistakes, Rax,' warned Mayhem, dangerously.

'I'll handle everything.'

'You'd better.'

Rax opened the map and looked at its strange markings.

'Now, then . . .'

'You'll have to triangulate from geological features,' urged Mayhem. 'That is, you'll have to use your head for something other than bowling!'

'Relax, Mayhem. I know what to do.'

Sly Rax climbed into Piranha's submarine side-car and pressed a button. He was launched into the canal at once. Mayhem watched as the machine slowly submerged.

Another VENOM master-plan had been put into operation.

Scott Trakker lay back comfortably in the gondola and relaxed. He reached out to take a bag of crisps from T-Bob's storage compartment and began to munch them. The robot had invented a novel way of propelling the craft. He was sitting on top of the tall, narrow, carved rear end of the boat with his legs telescoped out to maximum length. His feet just reached the water. Using them like paddles, he swung his legs in an exaggerated walking motion and the gondola sliced through the canal.

T-Bob was very pleased with his method of propulsion.

'This is much easier,' he said, airily. 'I don't know why the Venetians never thought of it.'

'Their legs are not as long as yours, T-Bob.'

'Nor as nice-looking!'

The gondola was now heading for a low bridge but T-Bob did not notice it. He was far too busy gazing around at the beauties of Venice. He indicated some houses along the water's edge.

'Think they have any rising damp?' he asked.

'Probably,' agreed Scott with a laugh. 'Boy, this is the way to see the city!'

'Yes. What a view!'

T-Bob suddenly had another view altogether.

He was staring at the low bridge as the gondola slid beneath it. Perched so high up, he had no chance of staying where he was. He was knocked over backwards and did a double somersault before hitting the water once again.

SPLASH!!!!

'T-Bob! Where are you?' wondered Scott.

Metallic hands gripped the side of the gondola and a dazed robot lifted himself out of the canal. He felt like the victim of a car accident and wanted a witness.

'Did you get the licence number of that bridge?'

'That does it!' decided Scott.

'Does what?'

'I'm going to tie you to the boat.'

'Why?'

'Because you've spent more time overboard than on board.'

Scott grabbed a rope that lay in the gondola and began to lash T-Bob to the vessel. He was determined to keep his friend in the gondola from now on.

'Do I *have* to be tied on?' bleated T-Bob.

'Yes. As a gondolier, you make a good anchor!'

'But it's so embarrassing to be roped up.'

'That's your fault.'

The robot continued to protest but Scott did not listen. He wound the rope around T-Bob to make sure that he could not fall overboard again. He wanted them to explore the canals of Venice.

But not by falling into them every two minutes!

Sly Rax was also engaged in exploration. The Piranha side-car was submerged beneath the water and moving steadily forward. With the aid of a pencil light, Rax studied the ancient map that had been

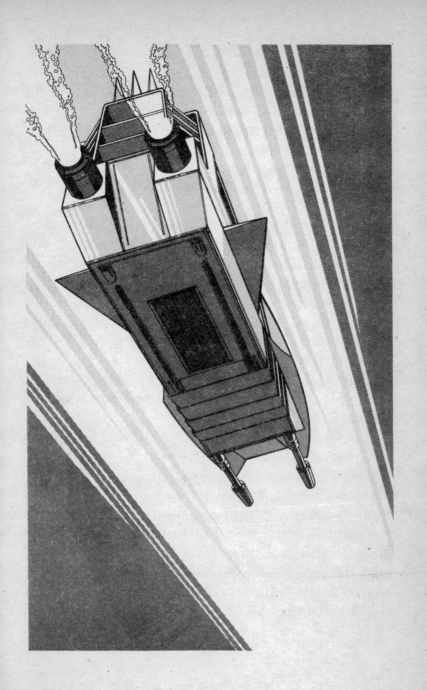

given to him by Mayhem. He glanced up through the windscreen.

'Water's so murky,' he moaned, 'I can hardly tell where I am. I better surface . . . carefully.'

He adjusted the controls and his craft rose gently upwards.

Rax did not spot the gondola directly above him.

It belonged to Scott and T-Bob.

'But I've got it all straight now,' argued the robot. 'Don't use the stick, don't jump into the boat, and watch out for bridges. You can untie me now, Scott. I know the Canal Code!'

'You're staying tied up, T-Bob.'

'Oh, no!'

'Oh, yes!'

'For how long?'

'Until you learn the ropes!'

Scott laughed at his own joke but T-Bob was very peeved.

'I'm safe now!'

'Safer still when you're tied on.'

'There's no way I can fall out!' insisted the robot.

His boast proved to be hollow.

At that moment, the submarine made contact with the gondola and tipped it up at a sharp angle. As the boat lurched violently, T-Bob was flung overboard with the rope trailing behind him.

Scott peered anxiously over the side of the gondola.

'What happened?'

T-Bob flailed about in the water.

'Eeeek! Piranha!' he cried. 'And I don't mean fish.'

VENOM had surfaced.

They had run into the worst kind of trouble.

FOUR

Scott Trakker began to haul frantically on the rope in an attempt to reel T-Bob in. He was only too conscious of the danger posed by VENOM. In his eagerness, however, the boy got tangled up in the rope.

'Hurry up!' yelled T-Bob.

'I *am* hurrying!'

'This is no time to get yourself tied in knots!'

Sly Rax stared through a window and saw the robot floundering past. He realised that there had been a collision and made a quick decision.

'Oops!' he said. 'I bumped somebody's boat. Better clear out.'

He adjusted the controls and Piranha sank again.

With a supreme effort, Scott hauled T-Bob back

into the gondola again but the loop of the rope was still hanging overboard. Piranha now zoomed forward beneath the water, snagging the loop on its rear end.

The rope was pulled tight. Since Scott and T-Bob were both tangled up in it, they were almost yanked overboard. The robot shrieked his protest.

'Not again! We're getting strung out!'

'I'll fix it,' said Scott.

Grabbing some of the slack, he swiftly twirled it around the prow of the boat. When the rope was pulled taut, it began to drag the gondola along so that the craft was cutting through the water like a speed-boat in a race.

Piranha powered its way on. Only the canopy was jutting above the surface. The tail and the snagged rope were below the water so Rax could not see them when he glanced over his shoulder.

He thought the gondola was chasing him of its own accord!

'Those clowns are following me! Gotta lose 'em!'

Rax opened the throttle to increase his speed.

The gondola was dragged even faster now and it became a real hazard to all the other traffic on the canal. It zigzagged its way madly past other boats and left a huge wave in its wake. Gondoliers yelled in protest and shook their fists angrily.

Scott and T-Bob could do nothing to save themselves.

They were thoroughly snarled up in the rope. The

boy tried in vain to release them but only managed to make it worse.

'I can't untangle us!'

T-Bob's arms were roped to his sides.

'And I can't reach my radio to call for help!'

They were helpless passengers on a runaway gondola. All that they could do was to hang on and hope for the best.

Sly Rax stole another glance over his shoulder.

'They're still chasing me!' he said in amazement. 'How can they go so fast.'

He looked back through the windscreen and saw a junction with another canal in the distance. Moving slowly across the intersection was a long excursion boat.

Sly Rax grinned as he saw his means of escape.

'That'll stop 'em,' he grunted. 'I can go under that boat – but *they* can't.'

He aimed Piranha directly at the pleasure craft.

The captain of the excursion boat was horrified when he saw the gondola heading straight at his vessel. He punched a button and sent out loud warning blasts on an emergency horn.

But the gondola seemed to take no notice. It came on.

Scott and T-Bob pulled wildly on the rope to no avail.

'I can't get it undone!' shouted the boy.

'You see what I see?' said T-Bob, trembling.

'We're gonna crash!'

'I daren't look!'

The robot covered his eyes and Scott tensed himself.

A crash with the large boat seemed unavoidable.

Matt Trakker and Jacques Lafleur were standing on the bank near Thunder Hawk. They had just been studying readouts on the vehicle's computer and they were comparing notes. Jacques spotted the gondola.

'Matt! Look!'

'It's Scott and T-Bob!'

'Heading straight for that boat!'

'Quick! We've got to save them!'

The gondola was less than a hundred metres from the crash now. Piranha submerged completely so that it would pass beneath the hull of the larger craft. Rax was convinced that he would be able to shake his pursuers off his tail.

Scott and T-Bob cried out for help.

The captain of the boat continued to sound his alarm.

Passengers crowded to the side of the boat and screamed, fearing that they would be injured in the crash. People on the bank yelled out as well.

Panic reigned everywhere.

Except inside Thunder Hawk.

Cool as a cucumber, Matt Trakker hit a button. A panel opened up at the rear of the vehicle and two guns emerged. Matt found his target on a video screen and fired.

A laser beam streaked across the water.

Meanwhile, a small, empty boat had drifted alongside the pleasure craft but it was not going to protect it from the impact. As the gondola surged towards them, the passengers became hysterical and scattered.

Calamity was about to strike.

Then the laser beam hit its target.

Zaaaap!

It cut straight through the taut rope that linked the gondola with Piranha. Scott and T-Bob were no longer being towed but their momentum carried them on. The speed of their approach turned out to be a blessing because it meant that their prow was sitting very high in the water.

The empty boat alongside the excursion craft acted as a perfect launching pad. When the gondola made contact, it skidded off it and soared into the sky. Captain, passengers and onlookers watched in awe as the gondola cleared the excursion boat before landing safely in the canal on the other side.

There was a huge splash and many people were drenched but that did not matter. Scott and T-Bob were unhurt.

The gondola floated gently on.

'It's Dad!' shouted Scott. 'He cut the rope.'

'He cut it pretty close, if you ask me,' opined T-Bob, trembling.

A great cheer went up from the passengers.

MASK technology had saved them from catastrophe.

Thunder Hawk was still parked outside the hotel where Matt Trakker and Jacques Lafleur had been joined by Scott and T-Bob, both of whom were relieved to be on dry land again. They reviewed the situation.

Jacques smiled at Scott and T-Bob.

'That was Piranha you fellows were playing whale boat with.'

'I know!' wailed T-Bob.

'VENOM's certainly got plenty of *pull*,' said Scott.

'Mayhem is up to something,' decided Matt. 'I bet that gelled water we found is connected with him somehow.'

'We need extra help,' suggested Jacques.

Matt nodded and switched on the computer. The monitor flashed. He gave his order into the microphone.

'Satellite link. MASK computer. Select MASK agents for mission in Venice, Italy.'

The computer whirred and bleeped then the screen image scrambled. When it cleared, the head of a young man appeared next to a graphic rendition of another MASK vehicle.

The computer's voice gave its information briskly.

'Recommended personnel: Calhoun Burns. Specialist in urban environments and structures. Vehicle code name – Raven. Amphibious capability essential for mission location.'

'Approved,' said Matt.

The screen scrambled again then a still of an attractive young woman came into view beside a computer graphic version of another machine.

The flat, functional voice continued.

'Gloria Baker. Champion race driver, black belt in Kung Fu. Vehicle code name – Shark. Submarine capability gives probable advantage. Selection complete.'

'Personnel approved,' replied Matt. 'Assemble Mobile Armoured Strike Kommand!'

As he gave the order, he pressed a tiny button on his wrist-watch and the liquid-crystal display began to flash. The signal would be sent across thousands of kilometres to the two agents.

MASK operated world-wide.

The lean, muscled figure of Calhoun Burns was in the stables when the call came. He was grooming a beautiful horse in a loose-box. His watch began to flash and the animal immediately reared up on its hind legs. Calhoun dodged the flailing hooves and dived through the open door. He closed and bolted the lower half so that the frightened horse could not get out.

Excited by his summons, he hurried away.

Gloria Baker was at the hairdressing salon when her watch started to flash. She was seated in a reclining

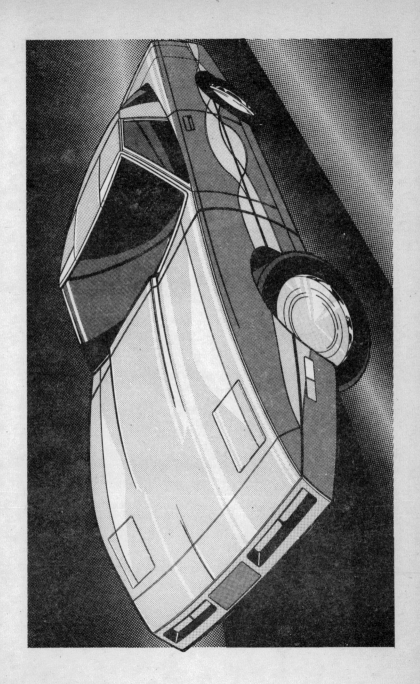

chair with her head leaning back into the sink as the hairdresser worked shampoo into her hair. Gloria responded instantly to the signal. Leaping out of the chair, she ignored the fact that soap and water were dripping all over her, and she ran out of the salon.

The hairdresser stared after her in sheer astonishment.

MASK business took precedence over everything.

The two agents soon met at the Boulder Hill gas station and went down to the energiser room in MASK's underground headquarters. They went through the familiar ritual then put on their masks and raced to their transports. Calhoun got behind the driving wheel of Raven while Gloria climbed into Shark. Both were remarkable vehicles with capabilities that made them ideal for this particular assignment.

They were soon roaring out of the gas station.

There was a long way to go but they would make it.

Neither of them had any details about their assignment but they sensed that it concerned VENOM. Miles Mayhem's criminal network had extended its operations to Venice. One of the most beautiful cities in Europe was at risk.

Calhoun and Gloria knew all they needed to know.

They accelerated together and rocketed on.

Sly Rax was still bewildered about the gondola that appeared to be chasing him but he tried to put it out of his mind. He was in Piranha for a purpose. Moving stealthily under water, the craft was searching for something that would be of immense value to VENOM.

Rax checked his map and kept Piranha on course. Its searchlights were on and its controls emitted sonar bleeps. A radar screen was peppered with small lines. Progress was slow but steady.

The submarine was not the only thing beneath the canal. It went past the wrecks of gondolas and other boats as well as sunken barrels, urns and general junk. It was another world beneath the water.

Rax became impatient when he could not find what he was after. He flicked a switch and complained into the microphone.

'Mayhem, this map must be bogus!'

'It's genuine!' insisted Mayhem's voice.

'There's nothing down here but hundreds of years' worth of old junk. The map must be a forgery.'

'Listen to me, idiot!' barked his master. 'That map was found sealed in an urn that was two thousand years old. It's genuine. I stole it myself. Keep looking!'

'It's a waste of time,' protested Rax.

He changed his mind in a flash.

One of Piranha's hyper-sensitive instruments tripped off an alarm.

An electronic beam started to glow on the dashboard.

'Hey, I got a reading!' said Rax with delight.

'What is it?' asked Mayhem, eagerly.

'It's big . . . it's metal . . .' Rax chuckled. 'This could be IT!'

VENOM had come to the end of the search.

FIVE

Excitement was high back at the VENOM hideout. Miles Mayhem, Vanessa Warfield and the burly Bruno Shepard were clustered around a portable communications console that included a television monitor. Nothing was showing on the monitor yet but they stared at the blank screen.

Rax's gruff voice was heard over the intercom.

'It's right where the map said it would be.'

'Of course!' replied Mayhem.

'Must be under the mud here.'

'Take a sonograph to read the shape through the mud.'

'Coming up, Mayhem.'

They heard some weird electronic bleeps then a

sonographic image appeared on the screen. It was a hazy picture made up of blurred grey tones but it was possible to make out the silhouette of a galley-style ship from ancient Egypt.

Miles Mayhem cackled with greedy delight and snatched up a drawing that lay beside him. He compared it with the image on the screen.

'That's it! That's it!'

'Let me see,' said Vanessa.

She took the drawing from him and examined it carefully. It showed an ancient depiction of Cleopatra's legendary barge with a high prow, full sails and dozens of oarsmen rowing on different levels.

Vanessa Warfield was overwhelmed by it all.

'Cleopatra's barge!' she exclaimed. 'It really existed! But how did it wind up in northern Italy?'

'It was stolen after Cleopatra's death,' said Mayhem. 'But the thieves were lousy sailors and lost it here in a canal.'

'Sounds like something Bruno would do,' teased Vanessa.

The agent shot her a nasty look that she ignored.

Vanessa held up the drawing next to the shadow-image on the console. They matched perfectly. She and Mayhem were convinced that they had located the right wreck. Bruno had his doubts.

'Looks like any other sunken boat,' he argued.

'Ah,' said Mayhem, 'but this boat is rather special.'

'Why?'

'Because it's made of solid gold.'

'GOLD!!!!'

Bruno had got the message at last.

The MASK vehicles were all parked in line on the street at the top of the boat-loading ramp. Raven and Shark were at the front, facing the water, while Thunder Hawk and Volcano stood behind them. As they glinted in the sun, the machines looked quite harmless. A casual observer would never have guessed that they each had such remarkable capabilities.

Matt Trakker, Jacques Lafleur, Calhoun Burns and Gloria Baker were all standing beside the Volcano van. They were in civilian clothes now and none of them wore their masks.

Matt gave the order to his specialist agents.

'Disperse and keep your eyes peeled for anything that looks at all VENOMous!'

'Dastardly devils!' said Calhoun in his pleasing drawl. 'They'll answer to us if they attempt to harm this grand old city. To our vehicles.' He checked himself and bowed courteously to Gloria. 'After you, of course, my dear.'

Calhoun Burns was a real gentleman. Until he was fighting VENOM.

Gloria thanked him with a smile then jumped into Shark. It converted to submarine mode, plunged into the canal and vanished within a couple of seconds.

Calhoun leapt into Raven and gave the command.

'MASK!'

His Gulliver mask came down automatically to cover his face. Raven converted to jet boat mode and skimmed over the water.

Jacques sighed his disappointment.

'I'm not going to be much help, searching Venice in a land vehicle like Volcano,' he remarked, sadly.

'Never mind,' said Matt. 'Just keep your eyes peeled.'

Matt climbed into Thunder Hawk and raced down the loading ramp. Just before it hit the water, it converted to jet mode and zoomed off into the sky.

The MASK team was on the alert. Thirsty for action.

Sly Rax had worked hard beneath the surface of the water. Having found the place where the barge was submerged, he had set a circle of remote-control, explosive harpoons around the area. He fired two more for good measure and they embedded themselves in the mud.

'Okay, Mayhem,' he said into his microphone. 'It's all set. I've got the harpoons in position around the barge.'

'Good,' said Mayhem's voice.

'What do I do now?'

'Get Piranha out of there.'

'Right.'

'Make it snappy!' ordered Mayhem. 'We're coming in soon.'

'I'm on my way now!' promised Rax.

He turned Piranha around and headed back the way

he had come. Sly Rax knew that he had to get out of the canal as quickly as he could.

It would be fatal to stay below water.

Back at the VENOM hideout, Miles Mayhem and Vanessa Warfield had gone up to the flat roof of the building. Their vehicles were parked there in readiness. Both had been equipped with crop-dusting spray rigs. Switchblade had a tank mounted on its undercarriage while Manta had one fitted to its rear bumper.

Extending horizontally from each tank were long, multi-headed spray jets for dispersing the gel fluid. The drum of fluid was mounted on a pivoting stand that moved on rollers.

Vanessa pushed it over to Manta and tilted the drum so that the purple liquid poured into its supplementary tank. While she was doing this, Mayhem spoke into Switchblade's radio microphone again.

'Bruno,' he snapped. 'Get into position.'

'I'm ready,' answered a rough voice.

Bruno Shepard was in Scorpion. The vehicle, still in street mode, was parked at the edge of the canal not far away. The water level at that point was only just below the bank.

'I'm as close as I can get to the barge by land,' said Bruno.

'Stay there,' ordered Mayhem.

The VENOM leader switched off and joined Vanes-

sa as she poured the gel fluid into Manta's spray tank. He allowed himself a boast.

'When the barge sank, no technology existed that could raise it. Eventually it was forgotten.' He grinned. 'But not by *me!*'

'Well done, Mayhem,' she congratulated.

'Finished yet?'

'Just about.'

Manta's tank overflowed. Vanessa shoved the drum stand away, leaving the drum tilted so that the excess fluid continued to ooze out of it. She went back to screw the cap on the spray tank.

Piranha, meanwhile, had arrived on the canal bank down below. Sly Rax converted the vehicle back to a side-car and screwed it on to the waiting motorcycle.

He called up to his colleagues on the roof above him.

'Hey, up there! I'm all clear!'

The fluid that had been pouring out of the drum now cascaded over the edge of the roof. Rax was soon covered in a gooey, purple liquid.

'Gaaaa!'

Unaware of what had happened, the two VENOM machines took off from the roof, Manta converting to a stealth bomber. Both aircraft flew low between the tall buildings of Venice.

Mayhem spoke into his radio microphone.

'Now, remember,' he said. 'Once we gel the water, we have less than an hour to pull this job off!' He paused. 'Mask!'

His Viper mask automatically came down.

VENOM was ready to work its evil yet again.

Matt Trakker was flying over the city and studying the picturesque panorama that was beneath him. His search was revealing nothing.

He switched on his radio microphone.

'My bird's eye view is laying an egg,' he admitted. 'Anyone else spot anything?'

Calhoun answered from Raven which cruised down a canal.

'I don't see a single unusual thing down here.'

Gloria replied from Shark which was gliding under-water past the aged foundations of Venice's noble buildings.

'Nothing *on* the canal,' she confirmed. 'Nothing *under* it.'

'Keep searching,' ordered Matt. 'I get the feeling that something might happen at any moment.'

The MASK agents stuck to their task.

Mayhem decided that it was time to spray the gel. Flicking a switch on the control panel in Switchblade, he activated the spray nozzles. The purple liquid rained down on the canal below him.

A couple of boats were moving slowly along in the water. As soon as the fluid hit the canal, it started to gel. The boats suddenly found themselves trapped in a morass of hard jelly.

Vanessa achieved the same effect in another canal.

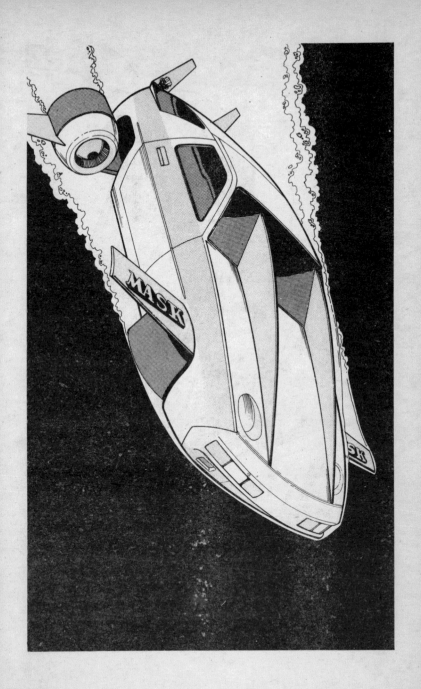

Manta sprayed the purple fluid and it gelled the water almost immediately.

Raven cruised along yet another of the many canals. Calhoun Burns stood up through the opening in the roof above the driver's seat. Switchblade came into view with its spray nozzles working away.

Calhoun spoke into his radio microphone.

'Matt, Gloria! It's Mayhem in Switchblade. I'm going after him!'

He gunned the engine but the boat was stuck fast in the now solid water. No matter how hard he revved the engine, he could not move.

'Okay!' yelled Calhoun. 'I'll pursue the vagabond on foot.'

He jumped out of Raven but the surface of the gel was very slippery and his feet skidded from beneath him. He could neither stand up nor get enough traction to walk along.

'This stuff's slicker than banana peels on ice!'

Gloria, meanwhile, was having her own problems with the gel. Shark was still underwater when the fluid took effect. She found herself and her vehicle trapped inside the clear substance.

'I'm stuck!' she protested. 'I feel like I'm in somebody's blackcurrant jelly.'

From his vantage point in Thunder Hawk, Matt Trakker could see that the whole canal system was seizing up. He knew the cause.

'VENOM's gumming up the works yet again!'

He sat back and gave a firm command.

'Mask!'
Spectrum descended to cover his face.
He was ready to tackle the enemy now.
VENOM had struck first. MASK could now hit back.

SIX

Scott Trakker and T-Bob stood on the steps that led down to the canal. The robot tried the water with a tentative foot and found it solid.

'Hey, look!' he said. 'The whole canal has gelled.'

His foot slipped from under him and he slid rapidly across the slippery surface. Scott laughed. T-Bob was equal to the emergency. He telescoped his arms and legs all the way out then stood on all-fours, looking like a strange, mechanical spider. With the improved traction, he could now walk quite easily. He demonstrated his locomotion.

'You may laugh,' he returned, 'but I think I can extend myself to meet this situation.'

'Great!' applauded Scott. 'You can give me a ride.'

'Your father warned us to stay off the canal.'

'Dad didn't say we weren't allowed to *walk* on it.'

'Okay,' agreed T-Bob. 'But somehow I feel your father won't exactly be thrilled by your logic.'

He took the boy on his back and walked over the gel.

Miles Mayhem hovered over Venice like a dark shadow and he was pleased by what he saw. His plan had so far gone without a single hitch.

'Every water vehicle in the city is now useless!' he noted. 'Scorpion – move in!'

He flew Switchblade down closer to the Grand Canal so that he could watch the other VENOM vehicle in action. The next part of the operation was a very critical one.

When he got the order, Bruno Shepard converted Scorpion to tank mode and opened the driver's hatch so that his head looked out. The vehicle started up and lumbered straight on to the gelled water.

Bruno gazed around with grim satisfaction.

'It works!' he shouted. 'Scorpion can drive right over this stuff! I'm the only one who can move around.'

With Switchblade hovering directly above it, Scorpion rolled slowly across the gel to a designated spot. Bruno checked a map to see that he was in position then contacted his colleague on the radio microphone.

'I'm ready, Rax. Fire the explosive harpoons.'

Sly Rax, wearing his mask, was now sitting in Piranha.

He still had splotches of the purple fluid on him.

'Roger!' he replied. 'Heads up out there!'

He reached out to press a button on Piranha's controls.

There was a terrific explosion as the harpoon darts were set off. Gigantic chunks of the gelled water were thrown up into the air, leaving a gaping hole in front of Scorpion. The hole had gently sloping sides and the canal mud was exposed at the bottom.

Scorpion headed down into the hole, its powerful claw arm extending downwards as it went. Bruno was enjoying his task.

Mayhem gloated as he watched from Switchblade.

'Just as I thought! The gelled water can't flow back into the hole.' His cackle resounded. 'It won't be long now.'

Thunder Hawk came flying across the sky.

Matt Trakker spotted the enemy aircraft and smiled.

'Let's add a little hot sauce to VENOM's pudding!'

His doors' lasers fired in rapid succession.

The beams sliced viciously past the canopy windows on Switchblade. Mayhem looked around himself in desperation. He saw who it was.

'MASK!'

Switchblade converted to jet mode and zoomed off.

Thunder Hawk gave chase, firing at random as it went. Then the MASK aircraft was itself attacked. Manta flew out from behind some buildings and started firing rockets at Thunder Hawk.

Matt looked over his shoulder and saw Vanessa Warfield.

'This game of tag is turning into leapfrog!'

He broke off his attack on Mayhem and swooped back down towards the city, cutting in between rows of buildings. Manta was in hot pursuit.

Matt notified his agents over the radio microphone.

'Got a feeling I'll be busy for a while. Try to get to the mouth of the Grand Canal. VENOM's digging something up there.'

Calhoun was still trapped in the gelled water.

'I should be there any year now,' he said, sarcastically.

He slapped Raven in annoyance.

Desperate to get into action, he was held firm.

Jacques Lafleur was still waiting at the loading ramp. He found a long pole and poked at the surface of the gel with it. When he had decided it was firm enough, he ran back to Volcano.

'I can't stand doing nothing! Let's risk it!'

When he got into the driving seat, he gave an order.

'Mask!'

His Mirage mask automatically covered his face.

Volcano converted to defence mode and charged down the ramp and on to the water. It skidded around for a while and its wheels threw up some large gobs of the gelled water. But the over-sized tyres did manage to get a grip on the gel. He was able to drive slowly.

'I'll get in on the action yet!' he said with a laugh.

Gloria Baker had the same attitude as Jacques.

Eager to be involved in the fight against VENOM, she hated the idea of being immobilised beneath the canal. She had not come all that way to miss out on the fun. She gave one last shove against the door of Shark but it refused to open.

Gloria's patience ran out. She slapped her thigh.

'The heck with this!' she exclaimed. 'I'm not waiting around here any longer.'

She was wearing her Aura mask and she gave it an order.

'Aura – on!'

Its powerful beam shot out at once and forced the door of the vehicle open. When it met the solid mass of gel, the beam intensified and gradually forced the substance apart so that a deep trench was created. As Gloria walked along the trench, the beam continued to make a path for her.

She was strolling along the bed of the canal.

It was like the parting of the Red Sea.

'I hope Moses won't be offended,' she said.

The channel eventually led her to some stone steps at the side of the canal. Gloria climbed up them and stood on the bank. She had escaped at last. All she had to do now was to find some alternative transport. She looked around.

Calhoun Burns had also lost his patience by now.

Having travelled from America to take on a deadly foe, he was sitting in Raven on top of what looked like a mammoth jelly. It was very frustrating. No matter

how hard he revved his engine, he could not move the machine.

Suddenly, Volcano rolled noisily towards him.

'Jacques!' he called.

'Looks like you're on the skids, *mon ami*,' observed Jacques.

'Raven won't fly.'

'Volcano can still erupt.'

'I'm stuck.'

'Can I give you a lift?'

'Please.'

Jacques offered his hand and Calhoun took it. Using all his strength, the French-Canadian pulled his colleague into the safety of the van. Volcano rumbled on.

'What about Gloria?' asked Calhoun.

'What about her?'

'Poor lady must be trapped under the water.'

'Not if I know her!' said Jacques. 'Aura will get her out.'

'So where is she?'

'We'll soon find her.'

They did not have far to look. As Volcano rumbled on down the middle of the canal, they saw the attractive figure of the female agent on the bank. Gloria motioned her thumb like a hitch-hiker to signal that she wanted a lift. Both men laughed.

Kicking up chunks of gel as it thundered on, Volcano headed towards Gloria as fast as it could go over the treacherous surface.

'Get ready to pull her in, Calhoun.'

'My pleasure.'

'Now!'

Calhoun leaned out of the passenger door and grabbed Gloria's hand. Gently but firmly, he hauled her into the cab of the vehicle and shut the door.

'Boy!' she said. 'Am I glad to see you two!'

'Time to track down VENOM,' decided Jacques.

'Just let me at 'em!' she asserted.

'Yes,' added Calhoun. 'I want a word with those varmints. I'll teach them to pollute one of the loveliest cities in Europe.'

'Venom would pollute anything,' noted Jacques.

'Take us to 'em!' urged Gloria.

Volcano headed towards the Grand Canal.

The conflict was long overdue.

Scorpion had now made its way to the bottom of the hole that had been produced when the exploding harpoons had been detonated. Bruno Shepard manned the controls and used the giant claw to dig away at the thick mud on the bed of the canal.

Still in helicopter mode, Switchblade hovered nearby.

Miles Mayhem watched it all with wicked glee.

'Hurry up, Bruno!' he ordered.

'I'm going as fast as I can.'

'We don't want this gel to melt on us.'

'What about MASK?'

'Forget them,' said Mayhem. 'Vanessa is taking care

of the MASK marauder. Trakker has got his hands full with her.'

'Good.'

The claw on Scorpion scooped up another load of mud and threw it aside. Both Bruno and Mayhem gasped. Something was gleaming at the bottom of the hole. It was a spar belonging to Cleopatra's barge.

And it was made of solid gold.

'We've found it!' shouted Bruno. 'The sunken treasure!'

'At last!' said Mayhem.

The claw worked fast to clear away more mud.

Part of the rigging came into view, then the bulwark, then the deck. In the bright sunshine, the barge was a thing of shimmering beauty.

Miles Mayhem thought only of himself.

'Bring it up, Bruno! I want it.'

'Okay.'

'It's worth billions and billions!'

'Yeah.'

'Do you see what this will mean?'

'Of course,' grunted Bruno. 'We'll have a nice golden barge to look at.'

'No, you fool!' roared Mayhem. 'We'll use the gold to finance our plans for world domination. With all that wealth at my disposal, nothing will be able to stop me. VENOM will triumph!'

His evil cackle echoed over the whole of Venice.

SEVEN

Scorpion was well-named because its sting was in its tail. The giant claw reached over from its tail and took a firm grip on the exposed spar. The vehicle's huge, tank tracks began to grind as it went into reverse. There was a great squelching sound and then Cleopatra's barge emerged from its resting place.

Bruno Shepard could feel the resistance.

'This must weigh fifty tonnes!'

'Keep pulling!' commanded Mayhem.

'It's sliding easily on this jelly water.'

'That was the idea,' boasted the VENOM leader. 'You know me. I always think of everything.'

'As long as you've thought of a way to keep MASK off our backs. We don't want them butting in on this.'

'They've got their hands tied, Bruno.'

'Great!'

'They won't be able to *barge* in on this!'

The two men shared a throaty laugh.

Switchblade then flew across to the canal bank where Sly Rax was waiting in Piranha. He was wearing his mask and there were still the glistening globules of the purple fluid on him.

'Rax!' called Mayhem.

'Yeah?'

'We got it.'

'I know. I'm not blind.'

'As soon as the barge reaches the bank, slice it up with your lasers. We'll take a piece in each vehicle.'

'Okay, Mayhem.'

'And be quick about it!'

'Right.'

'The sooner we get away, the better.'

'I bet the Venetians will be glad to see us go.'

'I'm sure they will,' agreed Mayhem with a chuckle. 'We knocked out their main tourist attraction. Who wants to come to Venice when its canals are all gelled over?'

'*We* do!'

'Yes, Rax – *we* do!'

Still chuckling, Mayhem took Switchblade towards the middle of the canal. The golden barge was almost completely free of the mud and its full size could now be appreciated. It was at least four times as

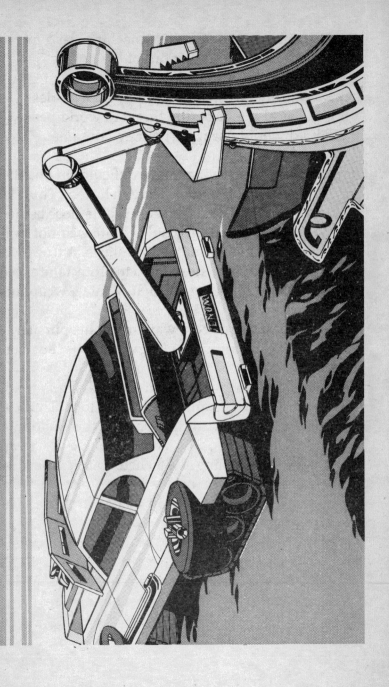

big as Scorpion but the VENOM machine was generating enough power to pull it out of the hole.

The sun hit the barge with dazzling effect.

It was a truly awesome relic of bygone glories.

But it was also a gleaming threat to world peace.

VENOM would use it for their evil designs.

Matt Trakker was having some difficulty in shaking Vanessa Warfield off his tail. Though he took Thunder Hawk along at top speed, she kept Manta close behind him, firing whenever she could. Matt was not only concerned to evade the bullets and shells. A true lover of architectural beauty, he wanted to protect the city as well so he had to make sure that Manta's weaponry did not destroy it.

Eventually, he spotted a way to lose his pursuer.

'This'll take all my nerve,' he admitted. 'But here goes!'

He was about to try some daredevil flying.

Swooping down from the sky, he took Thunder Hawk on a tortuous route between the buildings. Vanessa trailed him as he zoomed along a narrow canal, almost skimming the gelled water. Ahead of them was a very low bridge. If the aircraft went through, there would be only inches to spare. The manoeuvre demanded skill and daring.

'Come on, Thunder Hawk,' said Matt. 'You can do it!'

The MASK machine went under the bridge safely.

Vanessa Warfield, however, lost her nerve.

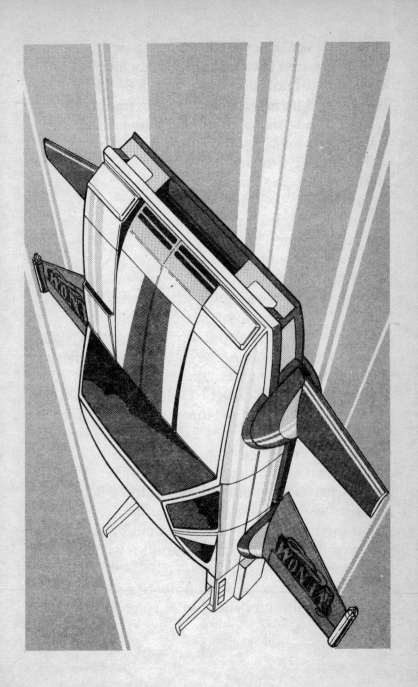

'No, thanks!' she yelled.

Manta soared back up into the sky and looped the loop. She had not been able to match the skills of Matt Trakker and he had finally got away from her.

Angrily, she snatched up the radio microphone.

'Mayhem!'

'I hear you,' growled her leader.

'I can't stop this maniac!'

'Trakker?'

'He's circling back in your direction.'

'Let him come.'

'Watch him – he's dangerous!'

'I'll clip his wings.'

Miles Mayhem was going to enjoy this.

Scott was still riding on T-Bob as the robot walked across the gelled water. They stopped when they saw the helicopter flying off to lurk behind a tall building. They soon saw why the VENOM machine was hiding.

Thunder Hawk came into view, aiming for the Grand Canal.

Matt Trakker was flying into an ambush.

'Look out, Dad!' warned Scott.

'He's behind that building!' shouted T-Bob!

'Switchblade is waiting to get you!'

But their voices were drowned out by the noise of the aircraft engines and their warnings went unheard. Matt was in the trap.

As Thunder Hawk dipped down over the Grand Canal, the helicopter sneaked out and fired its lethal stinger rockets. One of them hit the MASK aircraft head-on. Its hood was blown off and Thunder Hawk careered upwards with smoke pouring from it in a black cloud.

'Dad's in trouble!' said Scott.

'He's sending up smoke signals,' noted T-Bob.

'Come on!'

The robot galloped across the gelled water with the boy on his back. If Matt was going to crash, they wanted to be on hand to help.

High above them, Mayhem looked on with glee.

'That should occupy Trakker long enough for us to finish!' he asserted. 'Serves him right for trying to meddle with VENOM.'

It seemed as if Mayhem's plan was bound to succeed.

MASK had been vanquished.

Matt Trakker refused to accept that he was beaten. Though his aircraft was badly damaged and losing height quickly, it could still be put to good use. Matt gazed down from his cockpit.

Directly below him was Scorpion, slowly dragging the golden barge across the gelled water. On the canal bank, Sly Rax was waiting to slice the wreck into pieces so that it could be taken away.

'Thunder Hawk's about to become a lead balloon,' said Matt. 'So maybe I better make a real big splash!'

Scorpion continued to haul its mighty load across the canal. Inside the cab, Bruno Shepard grinned to

himself. He was pleased with the way things were going. VENOM was winning.

CRASH!!!!

Thunder Hawk landed only yards in front of him with a spectacular belly-flop. It skidded along and gouged a deep trench in the gel. Bruno saw that he now had a real obstacle.

'Oh, no!' he exclaimed.

'Go round!' ordered Mayhem over the intercom.

'Have I got time before it melts?'

'If you hurry.'

Bruno pushed a lever to get maximum power out of his engine then he guided Scorpion to the right. He went parallel with the trench, intending to go round it at the end. It would all add precious minutes to his journey.

Thunder Hawk had now screamed to a halt.

Matt Trakker climbed on to the roof and looked at Scorpion.

'Well, I stalled them,' he said. 'But now what?'

A loud, grinding noise swung his eyes the other way.

'Volcano!'

The MASK vehicle had come into the Grand Canal and was roaring along over the gelled water. Jacques was driving while Gloria and Calhoun were sitting in the gun positions. Laser cannons were soon blazing in all directions as the agents struck back.

Manta flew in overhead to be welcomed by a barrage of fire.

'That's *all* I need!' complained Vanessa at the controls.

She dodged away out of range as fast as she could.

Gloria was manning the upper turret guns on Volcano.

'Now for Mayhem!' she announced.

Lasers flashed into the sky all around Switchblade.

'It's getting too warm up here!' wailed Mayhem.

He swung the helicopter away to elude the attack.

Sly Rax watched it all from the bank and he joined in the battle at once. He pressed a button inside Piranha and started firing pulsed lasers at the MASK vehicle.

Jacques saw them coming and swerved to avoid them.

Volcano went into an uncontrollable skid.

'Hang on, everyone!' warned Jacques.

The heavy machine went spinning across the canal with its wheels throwing up whole sheets of the gelled water. A wave went over Sly Rax and helped to activate the purple fluid that still bespattered him. Before the VENOM agent could move, he was enveloped in a huge bubble of sticky gelatine.

He squirmed madly, trying to get out.

'Yaaaa!!!!'

Matt Trakker smiled in approval. He used his intercom.

'Good work, you guys!'

'Thanks, Matt,' replied Jacques.

'Calhoun.'

'Yes, Matt?'

'Use Gulliver. Make that barge a little easier to carry.'

'Roger!'

Scorpion had now reached the end of the trench. It made its way towards the bank of the canal where Piranha was parked. The golden barge gliding along smoothly behind it.

Volcano finally skidded to a halt. Calhoun opened the door of the cab and leaned out to aim his mask at its target.

'Gulliver – full power on!'

A brightly-coloured beam shot out from the mask.

When it hit the golden barge, its effect was immediate. The vessel began to shrink dramatically. What had once been a massive craft was soon only the size of a toy. It was far too small to be held by the giant claw and it dropped out on to the gelled water.

Bruno could not understand it.

'What happened?' he demanded. 'Where's my barge?'

He turned Scorpion around in a wide arc so that he could go back to the shrunken object. But his vehicle moved with laborious slowness. Someone else decided to race him.

Scott and T-Bob had seen the golden barge drop.

'Come on, T-Bob,' urged the boy. 'You can move faster than anybody on this stuff!'

'That doesn't mean I want to go,' said the robot, nervously.

'Ride 'em, cowboy!'

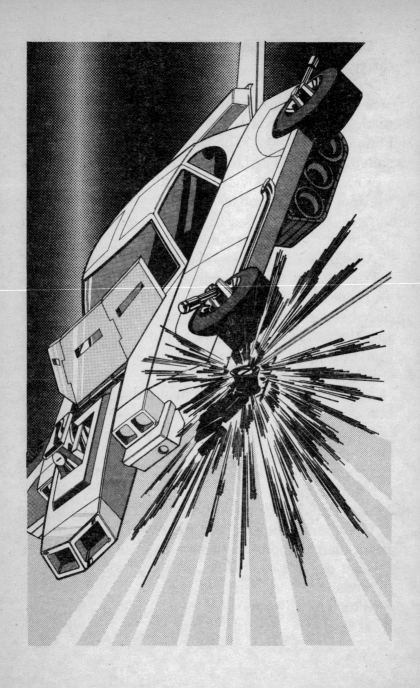

Sitting onT-Bob's back, Scott was taken across the surface of the canal at a gallop. Scorpion was closing in on the barge but the robot got there first. With great nerve, Scott bent down to scoop up the precious object as they charged past.

'I got it! I got it!'

T-Bob did not need to be told to retreat at top speed.

Matt was still standing on the roof of Thunder Hawk.

'Where did they *come* from? Cover them!' He aimed his mask. 'Spectrum lasers – fire!'

All its laser canons fired simultaneously.

Scorpion was unleashing its wheel lasers but its front tyres were suddenly shot out by the Spectrum attack. The VENOM vehicle came to a dead halt. It was out of the fight.

Mayhem observed it all from the hovering Switch-blade.

'Blast!' he roared. 'They've got the barge and it's a stand-off. Let's get out of here.'

Manta took his advice and flew away at once.

Bruno got on to the roof of Scorpion and waved for help. A few seconds later, the helicopter dipped right down towards him. As it swung past, Bruno grabbed hold of its runners and was lifted away.

Rax finally struggled out of the gel and raced off in his Piranha. The VENOM team had been put to flight yet again.

MASK had won through in the end.

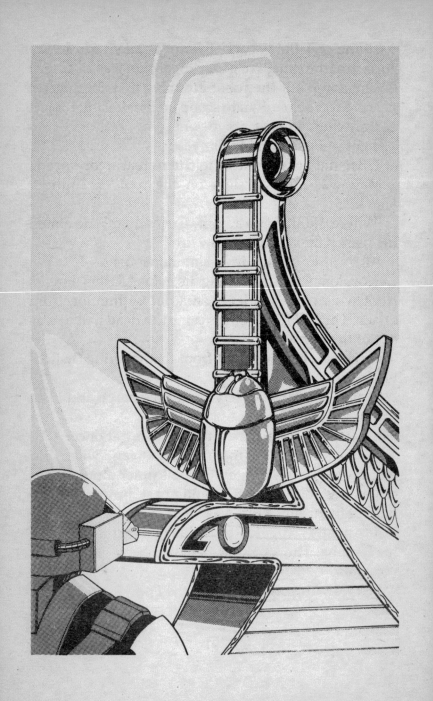

Matt Trakker and his agents stood in St Mark's Square with Scott and T-Bob. Volcano was nearby. Calhoun directed his Gulliver mask at the tiny golden barge and restored it to its normal size. Cleopatra's noble vessel towered over them with gleaming magnificence.

They had to shield their eyes from the dazzle.

'Amazing!' said Matt. 'It's thousands of years old.'

'That's how *I* feel,' sighed T-Bob.

'What happens now, Dad?' asked Scott.

'We'll take Cleopatra's barge to one of Venice's museums.'

'Yeah,' agreed the robot. 'And as far as I'm concerned, the *schooner* the better.'

They all groaned at T-Bob's excruciating pun.

If you have enjoyed Venice Menace, stand by
for . . .

MASK 4 – BOOK OF POWER
The revered Book of Power, holder of mystical and
ancient secrets, is sought by VENOM's leader,
Miles Mayhem, whose wicked intention is to turn
its magic to his own ends. The MASK mission is to
return the book intact to its rightful guardians, but
faced with VENOM's evil, the task is not easy.

MASK 5 – PANDA POWER
When all the Chinese pandas are stolen from the
nature preserves, MASK is not long in finding out
who lies behind the crime. Why a celebrated
sculptor should be kidnapped as well though, is
more puzzling and increases the alarm.

KNIGHT BOOKS

Five stunning MASK adventures from Knight Books

☐	39890 6	MASK 1 – The Deathstone	£1.95
☐	39891 4	MASK 2 – Peril Under Paris	£1.95
☐	39892 2	MASK 3 – Venice Menace	£1.95
☐	39977 5	MASK 4 – Book of Power	£1.95
☐	40327 6	MASK 5 – Panda Power	£1.95

All these books are available at your local bookshop or newsagent, or can be ordered direct from the publisher. Just tick the titles you want and fill in the form below.
Prices and availability subject to change without notice.

Knight Books, P.O. Box 11, Falmouth TR10 9EN, Cornwall.

Please send cheque or postal order, and allow the following for postage and packing:

U.K. – 55p for one book, plus 22p for the second book, and 14p for each additional book ordered up to a £1.75 maximum.

B.F.P.O. and EIRE – 55p for the first book, plus 22p for the second book, and 14p per copy for the next 7 books, 8p per book thereafter.

OTHER OVERSEAS CUSTOMERS – £1.00 for the first book, plus 25p per copy for each additional book.

Please send cheque or postal order (no currency).

Name ....

Address ....

....